This book belongs to

_____

This educational book was created in cooperation with Children's Television Workshop, producers of SESAME STREET. Children do not have to watch the television show to benefit from this book. Workshop revenues from this book will be used to help support CTW educational projects.

ON MY WAY WITH SESAME STREET™

Volume 13

In the City

Featuring Jim Henson's Sesame Street Muppets

Children's Television Workshop / Funk & Wagnalls

Authors

Linda Hayward
Michaela Muntean
Pat Tornborg
Ellen Weiss

Illustrators

Tom Cooke
Robert Dennis
Tom Leigh
Carol Nicklaus
Maggie Swanson
Richard Walz

A Parents' Guide to IN THE CITY

Learning about cities is an important part of beginning to understand geography and the man-made environment. This book shows your child what to expect in the city — what it looks like and what it has to offer. It introduces children to interesting city sights such as the museum, the zoo, and the park.

"The City Worm and the Country Worm" is a story about what happens when Slimey the Worm's country cousin, Squirmy, comes to visit him in the city — and what happens when Slimey goes to visit Squirmy in the country. At the end of the story, both worms agree that there's no place like home.

In "Who's Who at the Zoo," Big Bird introduces a favorite city sight and the animals who live there.

"The Monster Hall of Fame" is an amusing visit to the Monsterpolitan Museum. Your child will meet Vincent van Monster and other illustrious members of monsterdom.

"Construction Site," "Silly City Park," and "A Day in the City" are activities that show various aspects of city life.

The stories in this volume give some glimpses of life in the big city, and might give you some ideas for things to do if you and your child have the opportunity to visit the city.

The Editors
SESAME STREET BOOKS

The CITY WORM and the COUNTRY WORM

"Hey, Slimey!" said Oscar, holding up a thimble filled with water. "You're on." Oscar meant that it was time for Slimey, his pet worm, to practice his newest trick. "I can hardly wait to tell everyone about this," said Oscar. "I bet no one has ever seen a worm dive from a diving board into a thimble full of water."

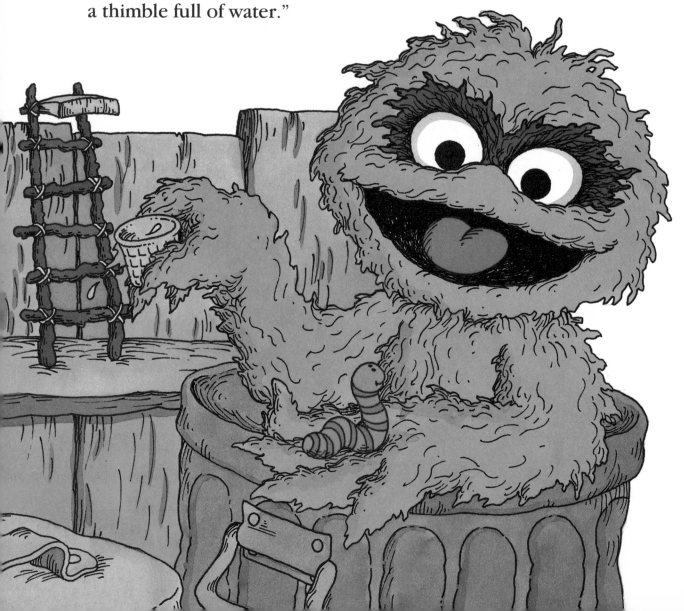

Slimey climbed up the little ladder. He wriggled to the end of the diving board and looked down. There was the thimble full of water. Slimey took a deep breath and dived. He landed in the thimble with a SPLISH.

"Terrific dive!" said Oscar. "A few more practice sessions and you'll be ready for the big time."

"Good," said Slimey as he toweled off. "And now I have to go tidy up my room. My cousin Squirmy is coming to visit me tonight."

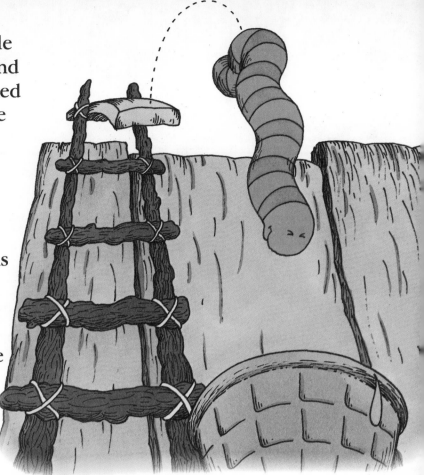

That evening Squirmy arrived with her suitcase. The first person she saw on Sesame Street was Oscar.

"Excuse me, sir," she said. "I am looking for my cousin Slimey. Does he live around here?"

"Yeah," said Oscar. "Slimey lives right there in that shoe box."

"Thanks," said Squirmy. "By the way, is it always so noisy in the city?"

Oscar looked around at Sesame Street. Cars and trucks were rumbling by. The garbage collector was rattling cans.

A police van sped past blaring its siren.

A rock band was practicing upstairs.

"What noise?" said Oscar. "I don't hear anything. When you live in the city, you get used to noise."

Just then Slimey wriggled out of his shoe box.

"Cousin Squirmy! How nice of you to come!"

"Cousin Slimey! It's wonderful to be here!"

"Welcome," said Slimey, "to the Big Apple."

"What apple?" asked Squirmy.

"Oh, that's just a funny name for the big city," said Slimey. "We call our city the Big Apple."

Slimey took Squirmy to his room and helped her unpack.

Squirmy loved Slimey's room. She admired his plants on the windowsill and his tie-dyed pillows on the bed and his I LOVE SESAME STREET poster on the wall.

The next day Slimey gave Squirmy a tour of the city. He took her to the Earthworm Museum. There they saw twenty different kinds of dirt in the Soil Sample Room.

They both enjoyed a colorful mobile entitled "Worm Turning in Slow Motion."

Slimey and Squirmy
ate their lunch at a
sidewalk cafe.

That afternoon they
climbed to the top of the
Sesame Street sign and
took in the view.

In the evening they
had front row seats at
the biggest earthworm
musical stage show in
town. (In fact, it was
the only earthworm
musical stage show
in town.)

"The city is a very
exciting place," said
Squirmy, "even if it is
noisy."

The next day it was time for Squirmy to go home.

"Thanks for everything," she told Slimey. "I hope you will come and visit me in the country."

"I've never been to the country," said Slimey. "Do you have a lot of museums and shows and sidewalk cafes?"

"No," said Squirmy. "We have a lot of quiet."

After Squirmy left, Oscar showed Slimey a sign he had made. "Isn't this a terrific sign?" said Oscar.

"I painted it myself."

"I didn't know that you could dive into a thimble full of water," said Slimey.

"I can't," said Oscar. "You are the diver."

"Then why does your sign say 'starring Oscar T. Grouch'?" asked Slimey.

"Because," said Oscar, "*I* made the sign. Heh, heh, heh."

"That is unfair," said Slimey. "I think I will go on a long trip. You can do the show without me."

As Slimey packed his suitcase, he wondered where he should go. Suddenly he thought of his cousin Squirmy.

"I know," he said. "I will visit Squirmy in the country. It will be nice and quiet there— no shows, no signs, no grouches."

Slimey went to the bus stop and waited for the bus.

When Slimey arrived at his cousin's address, all he saw was a big apple lying on the ground. Where was Squirmy's house?

He was very surprised when Squirmy poked her head out of the apple.

"Cousin Slimey! How nice of you to come!"

"Cousin Squirmy! It's wonderful to be here!"

"Welcome," said Squirmy, "to the Big Apple. That's what I call my house."

Squirmy lived in a real apple. Inside the big apple, there was a nice cozy room.

Slimey loved Squirmy's house. He liked the flowers on the table and the patchwork quilt on the bed and the HOME SWEET HOME sampler on the wall.

The next day Squirmy gave Slimey a tour of the countryside. They hiked through the crisp fall leaves. They went for a brisk dip in the local puddle. They even slept out under the stars. Slimey had never seen so many stars.

There was only one problem. Slimey couldn't sleep. It was too quiet.

"If only Oscar were here," thought Slimey. "He would make a lot of noise and I could go to sleep."

In the morning Slimey and Squirmy were talking about this and that when a robin flew up and landed on the branch of an apple tree.

Was that robin thinking about taking a nap? Was he planning to sing a song?

Oh, no! That robin was watching Slimey and Squirmy and he was thinking about only one thing.

BREAKFAST!

"This is the life," Slimey was saying to Squirmy. "No cars, no trucks, no garbage collectors . . . ."

Suddenly he looked up and saw a monstrous bird diving out of the sky, heading straight toward him! Slimey was too scared to move. But Squirmy was not.

She grabbed Slimey and pulled him into a hole in the ground. The robin could not reach them.

After the robin flew away, they came out of the hole.

"What was *that*?" cried Slimey.

"Oh, that's just Robin Redbreast," said Squirmy.

"You've seen him before?" said Slimey.

"Oh, yes," answered Squirmy. "You should see all the birds that live around here — robins and thrushes and chickadees. When you live in the country, you get used to birds."

Slimey decided that seeing one bird was enough. It was time to go home.

"I guess I'm just a city worm," said Slimey as he started down the road to the bus stop. "I like living in the city."

"And I guess I'm just a country worm," said Squirmy. "I like living in the country."

"Good-bye, Squirmy!"

"Good-bye, Slimey!"

When Slimey arrived home, he was surprised to see a sign hanging on Oscar's can. It said: WELCOME HOME SLIMEY.

The sign made Slimey feel good.

"Well, how's the wandering worm?" said Oscar.

"Tired of riding buses," said Slimey. "But I like your sign."

"Hey, if you think that sign is great, wait till you see my new sign for the show," said Oscar.

And he pulled out another sign.

"Well," said Slimey, "I guess I'd better start practicing."

Playing in the Park

Bert has brought his pet pigeon, Bernice, to the park to play with her friends.
What's your favorite game to play in the park?

jogger

tree

baby carriage

flowers

litter basket

sprinkler

Big Bird hides.

bench

lamppost

grass

pigeons

scooter

Grover falls.

roller skates

skateboard

tricycle

jacks

catch

stickball

jungle gym

barrel

slide

swings

jump rope

bicycle

Herry hops.

hopscotch

Cookie Monster jumps.

Prairie Dawn runs.

sandbox

seesaw

Ernie leaps.

tag

leapfrog

LOCH NESS
MONSTER

ROTTEN
APPLE
GALLERY

ABOMINABLE SNOW MONSTER

FRANKENSTEIN MONSTER

The Monster Hall of Fame

As the Mayor of Monsters, I welcome you to the Monster Hall of Fame. Throughout history, we monsters have taken monster-size steps in every field from science to sports.

Sadly, we have also had our share of rotten apples. Yes, even monsters sometimes do beastly things!

You have probably heard of our distant cousins the Loch Ness Monster, the Abominable Snow Monster, and the Frankenstein Monster. These monsters, who stomp about and cause problems, give us respectable monsters a bad name.

Here we have another rotten example. This is Cookie the Terrible. He cleaned out every cookie jar in Europe before he was caught red-handed in Chocolate Square!

I'm sure you have all heard of that great baseball player
Mickey Monster. He hit some monster-size home runs.

If you ever visit the Monsterpolitan Museum, you will
see paintings by our greatest artist, Vincent van Monster.
Here in the Hall of Fame, we are monstrously proud to
have his self-portrait.

The great scientist Madame Furry will always be
remembered for her contributions to monsterkind.
    Please remember the Hall of Fame monsters we have
seen here today. Great thinkers. Great artists. Great
monsters, all. *They* are the ones who make me proud to
call myself a monster!

Oh, I love to take a bath
When I'm feeling kind of grubby.
I just grab my Rubber Duckie,
And I hop into the tubby.

But bathing does remind me
Of another kind of treat.
The bubbles make me hungry;
They look good enough to eat.

RUBBER DUCKIE FLOATS

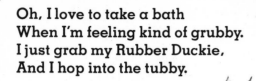

The water makes me thirsty,
And Duckie makes me think
Of a cool and frothy soda
That is both a food and drink.

So I'll fix a Rubber Duckie Float.
That's sure to quench my thirst
As it gurgles down my little throat!
But I'll finish washing first.

Note: Adult supervision is suggested.

Rubber Duckie Floats

To serve two—
What you need:
1 pint of lemon sherbet
½ cup of crushed pineapple,
   drained (save the juice)
1 tablespoon of pineapple
   juice from the can
1 small bottle of ginger ale
2 whole pineapple rings

What you do:
Put 2 scoops of sherbet, the crushed pineapple,
and 1 tablespoon of pineapple juice in a bowl.
Mix them with an eggbeater. Pour the mixture
into 2 tall soda glasses, and put 1 whole scoop
of sherbet in each glass. Pour the ginger ale
slowly into the glasses until the sodas become
sudsy. Don't let the suds overflow. Hang a
pineapple ring on each glass, and serve the
floats with a straw and a spoon.

A Day in the City

I know places in my neighborhood
Where I can go to get
A haircut or a hammer,
A pizza or a pet.
So get ready, get set, and let's go!
These are the places you should know.

Can you find a pair of scissors, a hammer,
a pizza, and a goldfish on this page?

Construction Site

plumb line

Mason

Hod Carrier

pipes

Plumbers   blowtorch

bricks

mason's level   mortar   trowel

scaffolding   Welder

hammer

Carpenters

sawhorse

light switch

electrical wires

wire clippers

outlet

Electricians

stepladder

Painters

paint roller   paintbrush

paint   drop cloth

roller tray   foundation

There's a new apartment house
going up on Sesame Street.
Big Bird is watching the workers.
Which job would you like to do?

girders

Architect

Foreman

blueprints

power shovel

scoop loader

crane

dump truck

bulldozer

cement

cement mixer

backhoe

Silly City Park

The park is the place for you to play.
You can run and swing on the swings.
But some people in this park
Are doing **silly** things!

Can you find seven silly things
in this picture?

Who's Who at the ZOO

It was a beautiful sunny day, and Big Bird, Ernie, and Bert went to the zoo.

"I can't wait to see the ostrich!" said Big Bird. "He's a big bird, too."

"I want to visit the pandas," said Ernie.

"Look, there are some pigeons," said Bert. "Oh, happy day."

"Mr. Snuffle-upagus asked me to say hello to his friend at the zoo," said Big Bird. He took a bag out of his backpack. "He asked me to give his friend these peanuts."

"Who is Snuffy's friend?" asked Ernie.

"Oh, dear!" said Big Bird. "I can't remember."

"Do you mean," said Bert, "that we're supposed to go see somebody, but we don't know who it is? How are we ever going to find Snuffy's friend?"

"Well, I do remember one thing Snuffy told me," said Big Bird. "His friend has four legs."

"That animal has four legs," said Ernie.

"That's a leopard," said Bert.

"Hi, Mr. Leopard," said Big Bird.

"But this is not Snuffy's friend," Big Bird said to Ernie and Bert. "Snuffy's friend doesn't have spots."

"Well, then, maybe it's that rhinoceros," said Ernie. "She has four legs, and she doesn't have any spots."

"No, I don't think so," said Big Bird. "I'm sure Snuffy would have told me if his friend had a great big horn like that."

"Here are the pandas," said Bert. "Maybe that one is
Snuffy's friend. He doesn't have a horn."

"I don't know," said Big Bird. "Look at those claws.
I'm sure Snuffy's friend doesn't have claws."

"This chimpanzee doesn't have claws," said Ernie.
"That's true, but he has hands," said Big Bird. "Snuffy would have told me if his friend had real hands!"

"Oh, there's the zebra. Maybe she's Mr. Snuffle-upagus' friend," said Ernie.

Big Bird thought about it. "No, I'm sure Snuffy would have said something about the zebra's black and white stripes. I don't think the zebra is Snuffy's friend."

"What about the giraffe?" asked Ernie. "Maybe he's Snuffy's friend."

"I think Snuffy would have mentioned it if his friend had such a long neck," said Big Bird.

"Oh, look, here's the ostrich!" said Big Bird. "Hello, Mr. Ostrich."

"I'm sure you're not Snuffy's friend," said Bert. "You only have two legs."

"And feathers!" said Ernie. "Hee, hee!"

"Wait a second," said Bert. "All you've told us about Snuffy's friend is that he has four legs. What else do you know?"

"Well, let's see. Snuffy said his friend had wrinkly skin," said Big Bird.

"Maybe he's a giant tortoise like that one over there," said Ernie. "I'll bet he even has wrinkles under his shell."

"I don't think it's a tortoise," said Big Bird. "I just remembered that Snuffy's friend has big ears."

"Big ears?" said Bert thoughtfully. "Maybe it's a rabbit!"

"No, it can't be a rabbit," said Big Bird. "Snuffy's friend is very big."

"I know! The hippopotamus!" cried Ernie. "He has four legs, wrinkly skin, and he certainly is big!"

"But," said Big Bird, "the hippopotamus does not have a snuffle."

"A snuffle!?" cried Bert. "You didn't say anything about a snuffle! We'll never find an animal in the zoo with a snuffle!"

"Look! Mr. Elephant has a great big snuffle!" yelled Big Bird.
"That's a trunk," said Bert.
"It looks just like a snuffle to me," said Big Bird. "And he has four legs, wrinkly skin, huge ears, and he's very big."
"Yes, but does he like peanuts?" asked Ernie.
"Let's see," said Big Bird. "Hi, Mr. Elephant. Your friend Mr. Snuffle-upagus sent you these peanuts, and he says hello."

The elephant grabbed the bag with his snuffle-trunk and dumped the peanuts into his mouth.

"The elephant is Snuffy's friend, all right," said Ernie. "He likes the peanuts."